This Book Belongs to

To Hiya Pari, my heart-fairy who is
always flying away from bed!
And to Ma, the soul-fairy who sang me lullabies.
With love and kisses – Toom-Ma

To Jaw & Dard – PC

Text copyright © Nandana Dev Sen 2016

Illustrations copyright © Pippa Curnick 2016

The rights of Nandana Dev Sen and Pippa Curnick to be identified as the author
and illustrator of this work have been asserted by them in accordance with
the Copyright, Designs and Patents Act, 1988 (United Kingdom).

First published in Great Britain and in the USA in 2016 by
Otter-Barry Books, Little Orchard, Burley Gate, Hereford, HR1 3QS
This paperback edition first published in Great Britain by Otter-Barry Books in 2017

A catalogue record for this book is available from the British Library.

ISBN 978-1-910959-02-2

Illustrated with mixed media

Printed in China

9 8 7 6 5 4 3 2 1

Kangaroo
Kisses

Nandana Dev Sen
Illustrated by Pippa Curnick

Otter-Barry BOOKS

Can a frog stand on its head?

"Darling, it's time for bed!"

Not yet!

"See your duck in the tub?
Won't you give her a scrub?"

Not yet!

My hippos in puddles need sleepy cuddles!

I'll snuggle Wild Whale,

and nuzzle her tail!

Then I'll **RACE** Alligator!

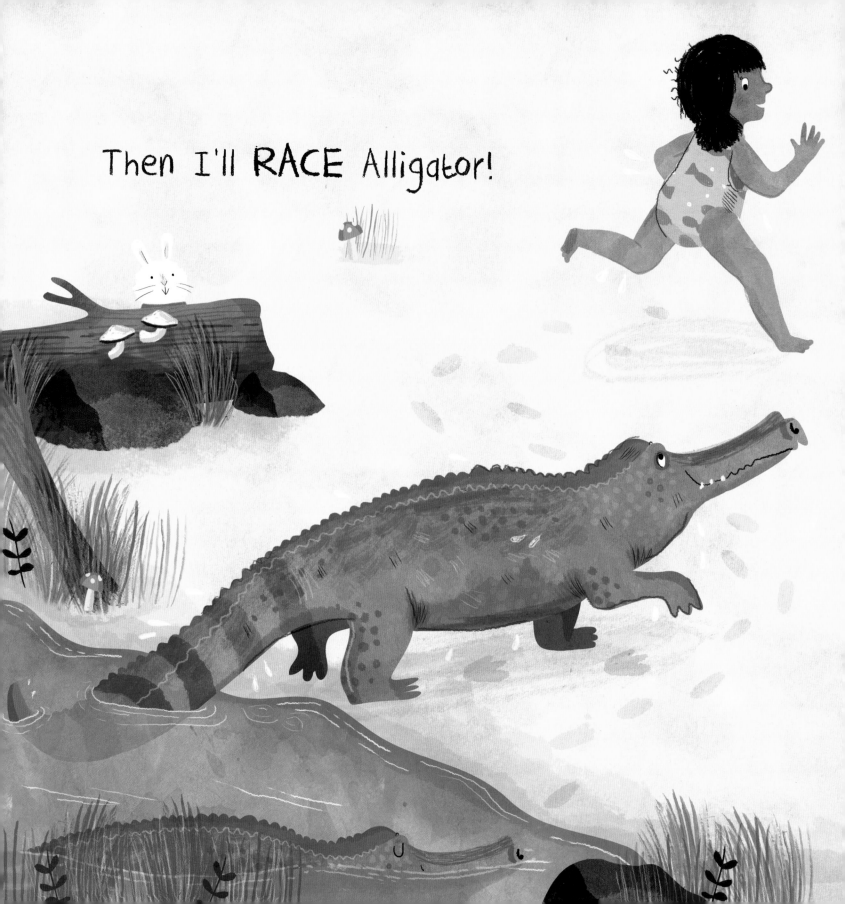

"No, chase him later.
Choose pjs - blue, pink?
And **please** have your drink!"

NOT yet!

If I **tickle** giraffe,
She'll **giggle** and laugh!

I'll sing with rhinos,
and dance on my toes!

"It's late, darling, **hush**!
Let's find your toothbrush."

Not yet!

Elephant must floss,
to make his tusk **gloss**.

Then I'll BRUSH furry Bear!

"Please brush YOUR OWN HAIR!"

Not yet!
See?
Monkey needs a **squeeze**...
she sleeps in those trees!

"See the clock?
Hear it chime?
You **know** it's bedtime!"

But I **must**
hug my pup!

"And I **must**
tuck you up!"

I will kiss Kangaroo!

"**NO**, now
I'll kiss **YOU!**

Will you turn
out the light,
and hug me
good night?"

YES!
I love you, I DO!

"And I love you too! Night-night!"